ABOUT THE BANK STREET READY-TO-READ SERIES

Seventy years of educational research and innovative teaching have given the Bank Street College of Education the reputation as America's most trusted name in early childhood education.

Because no two children are exactly alike in their development, we have designed the *Bank Street Ready-to-Read* series in three levels to accommodate the individual stages of reading readiness of children ages four through eight.

- ◉ *Level 1:* GETTING READY TO READ—read-alouds for children who are taking their first steps toward reading.
- ● *Level 2:* READING TOGETHER—for children who are just beginning to read by themselves but may need a little help.
- ○ *Level 3:* I CAN READ IT MYSELF—for children who can read independently.

Our three levels make it easy to select the books most appropriate for a child's development and enable him or her to grow with the series step by step. The *Bank Street Ready-to-Read* books also overlap and reinforce each other, further encouraging the reading process.

We feel that making reading fun and enjoyable is the single most important thing that you can do to help children become good readers. And we hope you'll be a part of Bank Street's long tradition of learning through sharing.

The Bank Street College of Education

To Rory and Kraig
—J.O.

COULD IT BE?
A Bantam Little Rooster Book
Simultaneous paper-over-board and trade paper editions/September 1990

Little Rooster is a trademark of Bantam Books,
a division of Bantam Doubleday Dell Publishing Group, Inc.

Series graphic design by Alex Jay/Studio J
Associate Editor: Gillian Bucky

Special thanks to James A. Levine, Betsy Gould,
Erin B. Gathrid, and Cheryl Dixon.

Library of Congress Cataloging-in-Publication Data

Oppenheim, Joanne.
Could it be? / by Joanne Oppenheim;
illustrated by S.D. Schindler.
p. cm. — (Bank Street ready-to-read)
''A Byron Preiss book.''
''A Bantam little rooster book.''
Summary: Surrounded by the many sounds of spring,
a hibernating bear is late in waking up,
until he hears one very special sound.
ISBN 0-553-05993-2. — ISBN 0-553-34924-4 (pbk.)
[1. Bears—Fiction. 2. Spring—Fiction.
3. Sound—Fiction.]
I. Schindler, S. D., ill. II. Title. III. Series.
PZ7.O616Co 1990
[E]—dc20

89-18258   CIP   AC

Published simultaneously in the United States and Canada

PRINTED IN THE UNITED STATES OF AMERICA

0 9 8 7 6 5 4 3 2 1

Bank Street Ready-to-Read™

Could It Be?

by Joanne Oppenheim
Illustrated by S. D. Schindler

A Byron Preiss Book

A BANTAM LITTLE ROOSTER BOOK
NEW YORK · TORONTO · LONDON · SYDNEY · AUCKLAND

[BEGINNING
READER]
Oppenheim

Once there was a big brown bear
who did not know it was spring.
He had been sleeping all winter long.
He did not hear the snow falling.
He did not hear the ice freezing.
He did not hear the wind howling.

He was sleeping snug and sound
in his den underground.

But one warm day
when springtime sounds
were popping all around,
something woke the bear.
What could it be?

Could it be the ice cracking
on the pond?
A fish heard that cracking sound.
But not the bear—
he was sleeping underground.

Could it be a bird singing?
A cat heard that singing sound.
But not the bear—
he was sleeping underground.

Could it be a cricket chirping
in the weeds?
A bunny heard that chirping sound.
But not the bear—
he was sleeping underground.

Could it be a frog croaking
on a log?
A duck heard that croaking sound.
But not the bear—
he was sleeping underground.

Could it be dewdrops dripping
from bursting buds?
A chipmunk heard that
drip-drop sound.

But not the bear—
he was sleeping underground.

Could it be a turtle snapping?
A fly heard that snapping sound.
But not the bear—
he was sleeping underground.

Could it be raindrops pattering
on the leaves?
A deer heard that pattering sound.
But not the bear—
he was sleeping underground.

Could it be tulips popping?
A caterpillar creeping?
A butterfly fluttering?
A worm wiggling?
Grass growing?
Or even a rainbow shining?
Could anyone hear these things?
Could you?

But something woke the bear.
Listen —*z-z-z-z-z-z-z.*
Could it be a buzzing bee?
Z-z-z-z-z-z-z.
Yes, it was a bee,
a fuzzy buzzing bumblebee,
that woke the bear!

And the bear knew that
where there are bees,
there is honey!

So he followed the
buz-z-z-z-z-zing bee
into the springtime world
of singing birds,
chirping crickets,
croaking frogs,
dripping dewdrops,
and snapping turtles.

He followed the bee through
pattering raindrops,
past popping tulips,
creeping caterpillars,
fluttering butterflies,
wiggling worms, and
a shining rainbow . . .
until he found the honey.

And it was as sweet
as the sounds of spring!

Joanne Oppenheim is the author of more than two dozen picture books, including *Have You Seen Birds?*, which won the National Picture Book of the Year Award in Canada. A former elementary school teacher, she is co-author of *Choosing Books for Kids* and is currently a Senior Editor for the Bank Street College Media Group. Ms. Oppenheim divides her time between New York City and her home in Monticello, New York.

S. D. Schindler has had a lifelong fascination with plants and animals. Studying nature is one of his favorite pasttimes. *Could It Be?* is one of numerous books relating to nature for which he has done illustrations. Others include the *Creepy Crawly Book* and *My First Bird Book*, which he also wrote. Mr. Schindler studied biology at the University of Pennsylvania and currently lives on three acres of woods in Philadelphia.